LOWRIDERS
to the
CENTER of the EARTH

BOOK 2

By CATHY CAMPER
Illustrated by RAÚL THE THIRD

chronicle books · san francisco

LUPE WAS A MASTER MECHANIC, AN IMPALA EXTRAORDINAIRE! WITH A WRENCH AND A RATCHET, SHE COULD REPAIR ANYTHING.

FLAPPY WAS A WASHCLOTH-WIELDING DYNAMO, PURO PODER* TIMES EIGHT!

ELIRIO PAINTED WITH HIS BILL. HIS BEAK WAS AS STEADY AS A SURGEON'S HAND, HIS SKILL IN DETAILING CARS UNPARALLELED.

4

* PURE POWER

* GARAGE ** CRAZY

* NEIGHBORHOOD **MARKET ***LIBRARY ****MILK CARTONS

"HEY, LOOK! GENIE'S PAW PRINTS. THEY'RE GOING TOWARD TOWN."

CLOSED
UNTIL WE FIND OUR GATO

Road trip! to find our lost gato.*

... my bag, Elirio's bag, and there's just enough room for El Chavo's things ...

... mis libros,** mis juguetes,*** my eight-legged pjs, my bowling ball, my guitar ...

El Chavo, you have to pick things that fit in your suitcase.

OK, but I *need* my guitar.

* CAT   **MY BOOKS   ***MY TOYS

* LET'S GO!

LATER . . .

. . . a la playa,*
to the shore . . .

What was that?

. . . lying in the sun, on my towel . . .

That sounded mean!

Wait, slow down, Lupe! We're headed straight for a cornfield.

16

* TO THE BEACH

* TO THE LEFT OR THE RIGHT?

* YES, THANK YOU!   ** SHORT FOR HOMEBOY, SOMETHING YOU CALL A FRIEND
*** MISTER   **** MISTER CAT; BUT ALSO A PUN: "SEEN YOUR CAT?"
***** HA HA HA!   ****** (IN RESPONSE TO A PUN) HOW DUMB!

* EYE

"–UNTIL DUSK,"

"DOWN INTO THE UNDERWORLD."

"BUT THE HEAT OF THE UNDER-WORLD POPPED XILONEN'S CORN, CONFUSING HER."

You lose, Cracker Jack!

Nincom-poop!

"MICTLANTECUHTLI FORCED HER TO BUILD THIS MAZE."

¡Pronto,* popcorn! I don't have all day!

"HE TRAPS CREATURES IN THE MAZE, CAPTURES THEM, AND FORCES THEM TO INHABIT MICTLAN, THE UNDERWORLD, WHERE THEY LIVE ON AS SKELETONS."

* HURRY

25

* HEH HEH HEH!

* THE VOLCANO   ** IT'S NOTHING; YOU'RE WELCOME

* LOOK AT ALL THE TREASURES!

* MURALS   ** MY HOUSE

* WAKE UP

These rocks got squeezed by the Earth and became new kinds of rocks.

You're so smart, Elirio. How come you know so much?

I collected palabras* when I was small. I put the ones I liked in my paintings.

* WORDS

"IT'S A WOMAN."

"SHE LOOKS LIKE SHE NEEDS HELP."

¿DÓNDE ESTÁN *MIS BEBÉS?**

We haven't seen any niños** anywhere, but we'll be glad to give you a ride.

We're looking for our lost cat. Maybe we'll find your lost kids too.

WAAA ¡Mis niños!***

* WHERE ARE MY BABIES?   ** CHILDREN   *** MY CHILDREN

* BUCKET ** TEARS *** A MONSTER, LIKE THE BOOGEYMAN, THAT PARENTS USE TO SCARE THEIR KIDS INTO BEHAVING

YEEII!
Lupe, stop!

It's El Cucuy,
he's after me!

What? Where
is he?

WAAA?
AUUGH
!!!

* DANG, NO WAY

* SANDWICHES

How can you tell? He's got sunglasses on.

Look at what he's drinking.

glug mmmm glug mmmm glug glug mmmm

Híjole, 'mano.* That hit the spot!

BAA!

BAA!

"¡SANGRE DE CABRA!*"

Yikes!

* WOW, BROTHER, OR WOW, MAN ** GOAT'S BLOOD!

* FAST

* IDIOTS!

* KITTEN

* HAM ** BRAVE *** ALL RIGHT

¡Imposible!* The knives are sticking to that hunk of junk?

* IMPOSSIBLE!

Genie, qué te pasó?* Is Mic trying to starve you into a skeleton?

We came as fast as we could.

.Mew! .Mew! .Mew!

Don't worry, old Miclanty-panty-con**-cooties won't hurt you any more!

I don't know how that bocina*** helped you out. And I thought I told you not to make fun of my name, Short Stacks!

How DARE you think you'll get your gato back just because you got through the Wind of Knives! There's something else you have to do first.

What? That was *not* part of the deal.

Fools! Bring that Wafflehead's bucket filled with water to the center of the Earth and back, and *then* maybe I'll consider giving your little kitty cat back.

total lies!

74

That's it? Just . . . bring down a bucket of water?

Sure, amiga!* Bring a bucket of water—into 6,000-degree heat!

Heh heh heh! A little hotter than a pizza oven.

Uh, what happens to, say, a pizza at 6,000 degrees?

The pizza combusts before it can even bake, Tortita!**

Pow!

This'll deep fry those punks and turn them all into chimichangas,*** mwajajaja!

Journey to el centro del planeta!****

¡Rápido!

* BABY ** SHELLFISH IN SOUP

* JUST LIKE THAT!

* DROP

Whaa happened? Did we make it?

Mi'jo, you've come back!

Homes, thank goodness you're OK! You were looking a bit seco.* Now your bucket is filled up!

Ahhh . . . salt water!

¡LAGRIMAS!

* DRY

* OVEN

* IN WRESTLING, THE BAD GUY OR BRAWLER

Running, plus my weight, plus bouncing off the rope at just the right angle equals ¡TRIUNFO!*

Oh no!

Giddy up, Impala!

FLIP!

* TRIUMPH!

* BUTT ** A LICENSE PLATE; SLANG FOR A TATTOO ON
THE LOWER BACK *** SPANKING

* GIRL ** FARTS *** MY EYES!

* DON'T BE RIDICULOUS! ** PUNKS

* LIKE A BOWLING BALL. ** PARTY!

* AY YA YA YAY SING AND DON'T CRY! A LINE FROM THE POPULAR SONG "CIELITO LINDO."   ** I AM LIKE THE GREEN CHILE, LLORONA, SPICY BUT TASTY. A LINE FROM THE FOLK SONG "LA LLORONA."

115

* WELL, THE VOLCANO ** LOWRIDER *** FAMILY

* I LOVE YOU SO MUCH.

* WHAT BEAUTIFUL MUSIC!

WHAT DOES IT MEAN / ¿QUE SIGNIFICA?

¿A la izquierda o la derecha?—To the left or the right?

a la playa—to the beach

amiga/amigo—friend

¡Ándale!—Come on!

¡Así mero!—Just like that!

¡Ay no, mi hijo!—Oh no, my son!

¡Ay ya ya yay canta y no llores!—Ay ya ya yay sing and don't cry! A line from the popular song "Cielito Lindo."

bajito y suavecito—low and slow

barrio—neighborhood

bebé—baby

biblioteca—library

bocina—speaker

bueno—good

cartones de leche—milk cartons

chale—dang, no way

chamacos—pip-squeaks

chica—girl

chimichangas—deep-fried burritos

¡Chispitas!—Sparks!, used as an exclamation

choners—underpants

Chupacabra [chew-puh-CAW-bra]—Also known as the goat sucker, the chupacabra is a dog-like monster with red eyes, known throughout Central and South America and the Caribbean for attacking cattle and livestock.

cola—butt

como una pelota de boliche—like a bowling ball

con—with

cubeta—bucket

¡Dame mi sombrero, stupid pollo!—Give me my hat, stupid chicken!

de nada—it's nothing; you're welcome

del mar—of the sea

despiértate—wake up

Día de los Muertos—Day of the Dead

¿Dónde está mi hijo?—Where is my son?

¿Dónde están mis bebés?—Where are my babies?

el centro del planeta—the center of the planet

El Chavo Pulpo—Octopus Guy

El Cucuy [el coo-COO-ee]—a monster, like the boogeyman, that parents use to scare their kids into behaving; the monster that hides under your bed

el rudo—literally, the rude one; in wrestling, the bad guy or brawler

el volcán—the volcano

¡Elote!—Corncob!

¡Exacto!—Exactly!

exoskeleton—on insects, a tough outer shell like armor that protects them

familia—family

gatito—kitten

gato—cat

¡GOL!—GOAL!

gota—drop

híjole, 'mano—wow, brother or wow, man

homes—short for homeboy, something you call a friend

horno—oven

hueco—hollow

Huehuecoyotl [way-way-coh-YO-tul]—the Aztec trickster coyote god

huesos—bones

¡Idiotas!—Idiots!

igneous rock—rock formed by hardened lava and magma, often associated with volcanoes

¡Imposible!—Impossible!

insecto—insect

¡Ja ja ja!—Ha ha ha!

jamón—ham

¡Je je je!—Heh heh heh!

La Llorona [la yo-RO-na]—a ghostly woman fated to search for her dead children forever, crying loudly wherever she goes

La Manopla—literally, the mitten; in Luche Libre in the Dominican Republic, a wrestling move; also, cheating by using brass knuckles

lágrimas—tears

liga—rubber band

loca/loco—crazy

lodestone—a kind of mineral that's naturally magnetic

los soniditos de mi amigo—my friend's little sounds, purrs

los técnicos—literally, the technicians; in wrestling, the good guys

Lucha Libre—professional wrestling in Mexico and other countries in Central and South America and the Caribbean

magma—molten rock

¡¿Maíz gigante?!—Giant corn?!

marisco in sopa—shellfish in soup

¡Máscara contra antennae!—Mask versus antennae!

¡Máscara contra cabellera!—literally, mask versus hair; in Lucha Libre, a masked wrestler versus one with hair instead of a mask

mercado—market, store

metamorphic rocks—rocks that changed into their current form because of intense pressure in the Earth

mi casa—my house

¡Mi chiquito!—My baby!

mi hijo/mi'jo—my son

Mictlantecuhtli [mick-lan-te-COOT-lee]—Aztec god of the underworld, who rules over all that die of natural causes. The Aztecs believed that a wind of knives ripped off the skin of the dead, who then lived with him as skeletons.

¡Miren todos los tesoros!—Look at all the treasures!

¡Mis amigos!—My friends!

mis libros—my books

mis juguetes—my toys

¡Mis niños!—My children!

¡Mis ojos!—My eyes!

moscas—flies

murales—murals

nalgada—spanking

niños—children

¡No seas ridículo!—Don't be ridiculous!

no te preocupes—don't worry

¡Nunca más!—Never more!

obsidian—a volcanic glass formed when lava cools rapidly, which was used by the Aztecs for arrows, knives, and other tools

ojo—eye

órale—all right

¡Pachanga!—Party!

pachucos—punks

palabras—words

pedos—farts

pelo—hair

¿Pero cómo?—But how?

pronto—hurry

pues—well

puro poder—pure power

¡Qué bárbaro!—An expression in response to a bad pun, like in English, someone would say "How awful!" or "How dumb!"

¡Qué calor!—That heat!

¡Qué chido!—Cool!

¿Qué hace el pez? ¡Nada!—A pun: What do fish do? Nothing! (The word nada means "nothing" but it also means "swim.")

¡Qué linda música!—What beautiful music!

¿Qué pasa aquí?—What's going on here?

¿Qué te pasó?—What's happened to you?

¿Quién ponchó mis llantas?—Who punctured my tires?

¿Quién sigue?—Who's next?

ranfla—lowrider

rápido—fast

¡Sangre de cabra!—Goat's blood!

seco—dry

sedimentary rocks—rocks formed by hardened sand and mud, often at the bottom of oceans, rivers, or other bodies of water

señor—mister

Señor gato—A pun: In Spanish it means "Mister cat," but in English it sounds like you're saying: Seen your cat?

¡Sí, gracias!—Yes, thank you!

sigan los murciélagos—follow the bats

socorro—help

stalactite—pointed piece of rock that hangs from the roof of a cave, formed by mineral-rich water dripping over many years

swamp cooler—an old fashioned type of cooler used in cars that allows hot air to flow over water to cool the air

taller—garage

tatuajes—tattoos

te quiero mucho—I love you so much

ten cuidado por favor—be careful please

Tepeyollotl [teh-puh-yo-LOT-ull]—the Aztec Jaguar god, who rules over animals, darkened caves, echoes, and earthquakes

tortas—sandwiches

tortita—little cake, pancake

¡Triunfo!—Triumph!

¡Un terremoto!—An earthquake!

una placa—a plate, in this case, a license plate. Tattoos on the lower back are sometimes referred to as license plates.

valiente—brave

¡Vámonos!—Let's go!

vato/vatos—dude, guy/dudes, guys

Xilonen [shel-OH-nen]—the youthful Aztec goddess of corn and fertility

Yo soy como el chile verde, Llorona Picante pero sabroso—I am like the green chile, Llorona, spicy but tasty. A line from the folk song "La Llorona."

¡Yo soy El Centro!—I am The Center!

¡Yo soy el mero mero!—I am the one and only!

DEDICATIONS

In remembrance of my big orange gato, Jambi, and to all my family and friends, here and in the land of Mictlan. —**Cathy Camper**

To Juaritos Lindo, el Noa Noa, JuanGa, y los ciudadanos de El Paso, Tejas. —**Raúl the Third**

ACKNOWLEDGMENTS

¡MUCHAS GRACIAS!—Diana Miranda and Violeta Garza—who read it first!

A big hand to Ana Schmitt and Ferner O. Bodden for La Manopla.

Many thanks to Mat Johnson and the VONA community for help and support.

Thanks to: Matty Monaghan, Omar the buff tiger, Raúl Gonzalez III, Delia Palomeque Morales, Diana Nunez, Byrd, Josh Rodriguez, Lucy Iraola, Mary Conde, Anne Seeman, Cynthia Cowen, Laura Jones, Sara Ryan, Rob Kirby, John Capecci, Amy Sedaris, El Vez, Davy Rothbart, Jon Scieszka, Megan McDonald, David Henry Sterry and Arielle Eckstut (The Book Doctors), Reforma Folks and WOC Zine friends, Roberto Y. Hernandez—your ride is awesome!, Jennifer Laughran, Ginee Seo, Taylor Norman, Neil Egan, Lara Starr, Jaime Wong, Sally Kim, and all the other wonderful people at Chronicle Books, Multnomah County Library staff and resources, my family, and everyone else who believed in and supported this road trip!

Many thanks to *Science Made Stupid*, by Tom Weller, for Flappy's geological knowledge. For more information about this book, go to http://tweller.com/. To read it online: http://www.chrispennello.com/tweller/. —C. C.

Thanks to Elaine Bay and Raúl El Gonzalez IV, my two loves!! . . . and to Dave O., Ruben and Danny G., Jennifer Laughran, Question Mark and the Mysterians, every one of my students, Ginee Seo, Taylor Norman, Caleb Neelon, Leo Espinosa, Karen Moss, and Joseph Carroll. Special thanks to my Art Director, Neil Egan, for keeping me on track and putting all the pieces together! —R

For a list of sources and works cited, please visit www.chroniclebooks.com/lowridersinspace.

AUTHOR'S NOTE

The Aztec religion was complex and included over two hundred gods. Part of their religion involved human sacrifice, to ensure that the rhythms and cycles of nature and the world would continue undisturbed. If a person died a normal death, it was believed they passed through nine layers of the underworld, including a wind of knives that stripped their flesh from their bones. They continued as skeletons to the land of Mictlan, ruled by Mictlantecuhtli, the Aztec god of the underworld.

The Aztecs had many scientific and technological skills, including astronomy and herbal medicine. They were also skilled stone sculptors, although much is unknown about their stone quarries and their stone carving techniques. Their stone sculptures were mainly carved of igneous rocks like andesite, diorite, and basalt—rocks found in the volcanic countryside where they lived.

Tepeyollotl is the Jaguar god, who rules over animals, darkened caves, echoes, and earthquakes. His spotted coat was supposed to represent the stars in the sky.

Coyote is a trickster who enjoys playing tricks and pranks in both ancient Aztec culture and in the beliefs of native Southwest American people. The Aztec god Huehuecoyotl, whose name means "very old coyote," enjoyed playing tricks too, and was also the god of storytelling, music, dance, and merriment.

Xilonen is the young Aztec goddess of maize, or corn, and fertility, who holds cobs of corn in her hands. In her more mature form, she is known as Chicomecoatl.

La Llorona, or "The Weeping Woman," is a ghostly woman who wanders the Mexican countryside looking for her lost children, and crying out "Ay mis hijos!" ("Oh my children!").

Chupacabra—the goat-sucker—is a monster known throughout Central and South America and the Caribbean. Mysterious incidences of dead livestock are often blamed on Chupacabra, who is thought to look somewhat like a mangy dog with spines down its back and glowing red eyes.

El Cucuy is like the boogeyman in the United States. "El Cucuy will get you if you don't stop that now!" parents might say to get their children to behave. Like the boogeyman, he doesn't have a specific shape, but people imagine him hiding under beds and in dark closets, waiting to pounce.

Lucha Libre means "free fighting" and is the name for professional wrestling in Mexico and other Spanish speaking countries in Central and South America and the Caribbean. Luchadores who wear masks are called *máscara*. They may be *rudos* (bad guys or brawlers) or *técnicos* (good guys, literally technicians). A fight between a masked fighter and an unmasked fighter is called *máscara contra cabellera* ("mask versus hair"). When losing a match, the ultimate humiliation for a masked fighter would be to have his mask removed in public, while, for an unmasked luchador, a loss would result in him having to shave his head.

Mictlantecuhtli, the Aztec god of the underworld, was one of the major Aztec gods. With his wife, Mictecacíhuatl, he ruled the underworld. He's often portrayed as a skeleton, with his liver dangling inside his ribcage, and wearing a skull mask, necklaces of eyeballs, and bone ear plugs. He has curly dark hair and penetrating eyes that allow him to see in the dark. He's associated with spiders, owls, and bats.

Day of the Dead/Día de los Muertos takes place November 1 and 2 and is celebrated in Mexico and many Latin American countries. In this celebration, which goes back to pre-Columbian times, people lovingly remember relatives and friends who have died. Altars, or *ofrendas*, are made in honor of the deceased, and are decorated with marigolds, *papel picados* (tissue paper stencils), sugar skulls, papier-mâché skeletons, foods and drinks the person loved, and, for children, toys they played with. Gravesites are cleaned and decorated, and often families and friends will stay all night in the cemetery visiting with the deceased. Day of the Dead parades feature large crafted skeletons, masks, and people in elaborate skeleton costumes. The parades sometimes lead to cemeteries and are themselves a kind of moving, living altar to those departed and remembered.

This book was written to celebrate the artistry, inventiveness, mechanical aptitude, resilience, and humor that is all a part of lowrider culture. We were also greatly inspired by Aztec art, stories, and the codices which recorded Aztec culture, in creating this graphic novel.

Library of Congress Cataloging-in-Publication Data available.

ISBN 978-1-4521-2343-1 [hardcover]
ISBN 978-1-4521-3836-7 [paperback]

Manufactured in China.

MIX
Paper from responsible sources
FSC
www.fsc.org FSC™ C008047

Design by Neil J. Egan III.
Additional typesetting by Liam Flanagan, Lisa Schneller, and Tara Creehan.
Typeset in Comicraft Hedge Backwards, P22 Posada, and ITC Century.

10 9 8 7 6 5 4 3 2 1

Chronicle Books LLC
680 Second Street
San Francisco, CA 94107

Chronicle Books—we see things differently. Become part of our community at www.chroniclekids.com.